HOLD ME UP IN MIGHTY WATERS

BY
KAYLEE JUKICH-FISH

TO ORDER ADDITIONAL COPIES OF:

BY
KAYLEE JUKICH-FISH

VISIT:

WWW.SCOTTPUBLISHINGCOMPANY.COM/STORE

SCOTT COMPANY PUBLISHING
P.O. Box 9707 • Kalispell, MT 59904
Toll Free: 1-800-628-0212
Fax: 1-406-756-0098

"We are all passengers on the *Titanic*,"

-Jack Foster, an Irish philosopher

This copy has been made especially for you. It has been created for only a handful of those closest to me to enjoy as a gift and an expression of my love and gratitude. Thank you for supporting me in all my endeavors. There's nothing I can put into words that can explain how deeply grateful I am to have you in my life. So I'm giving you a small piece of myself that is wrapped up within these pages.

With much love,
Kaylee

I

Mother, I will see you shortly. I am
devastated and heartbroken to hear of –

No no, that won't do at all. I crumple up the paper and toss it into the wire wastebasket next to the desk. That's the fifth attempt that I've discarded. It's been so long, I'm not sure what to say. I pull out another piece and try again.

Mother, I am en route to New York.

I hover the pen over my handwriting. There. Short, simple and it leaves no room for discrepancies… I hope. It shouldn't be this taxing to send a telegram. I dab my forehead with my coat sleeve, wiping away the pent up nerves that have escaped through my temples. Should I sign my name? Is that too formal? She will know exactly who this is from when she gets it. This isn't difficult and I should stop fussing.

"Frederick, are you still here?" The silvery tone of Jack Phillips startles me.

"Ah, yes," I try to use a hoarse, non-frantic voice, "Will

you send off this message for me? It's a little urgent."

I hand it to him and he scans it over.

"How urgent is a love note to your mother?" He chuckles and drops the letter on top of a growing heap of other, equally urgent telegrams. I feel my cheeks burn and stifle the urge to look down at my boots.

"You're right," I force laughter, "Just trying to get special treatment."

"Even if I wanted to, the telegraph is down. We can't send or receive a thing."

At that moment, the door flings open with a crash and a small curly-haired boy stumbles in, a box of metal… parts in his arms. Harold Bride, the junior wireless operator, sets them on the floor with a thump, his toothy grin spread ear to ear.

"Not for long," He says, brushing the hair out of his eyes, "We're going to fix it!"

"Are we now?" Jack, the senior operator, replies. "That's a direct violation of White Star Line's policy."

Harold appears sheepish and his smile falls.

"Those dingbats in the office don't know a thing about these machines. And if we pull into harbor with broken equipment - brand new equipment - they'll have our arses." Jack grumbles.

"So…" Harold edges on, a glimmer of excitement returning to his young wide eyes.

"So yeah, we're going to fix it."

Although Jack tries not to allude to his anticipation, his change of tone and small smile gives it away. He's rather young for a senior operator. Twenty-five, the same age as myself, and doing a lot better than my position as a… deckhand? Yes! A deckhand. My employment title almost slipped my head for a moment.

"You should get back to work, Frederick." Jack turns to me, "I'll send your message first if you promise to keep our mechanical experimentation on the hush."

"Of course," I wink and start for the door, giggling to myself as I watch the two young men dig through the various tools as if it was Christmas Day.

The thick scent of salt fills my nostrils upon exiting onto the boat deck. There is a light breeze that catches the bill of my cap, I klatch on to prevent it floating over the railing into the sea. The sun is halfway under the ocean now, casting brilliant orange rays across the water. As the swells catch the sunlight, they sparkle and dance over each other. It's peaceful. A wonderfully calm tide - the sunset indicating the end of my shift. Not that they keep strict tabs on us anyway. Hardly notice my absence or otherwise inadequate knowledge of nautical life.

The crew quarters are located deep in the bow of the ship, far out of sight of the prestigious aristocrats. Multi-millionaire's pace the halls of this floating castle, and it would be a travesty if any were to glimpse those in the working class. We are separated by both status, and an intricate hallway designed to keep us as far apart as possible.

It goes without mention that we are not allocated much space. Metal bunk beds stacked three high are crammed so tight together that even a person as skinny as myself has to shimmy in between. My bunk is visually set apart from all the rest. It's the only one that is neatly made with tomorrow's clothing folded at the foot. The rest of the beds are strewn about in tangled chaos. Dirty articles are mixed with clean, bed sheets crumpled into piles. I pity the poor wives who have to clean up after these men.

In the far corner, a group of roughly six men are laying in the bunks with a pile of coin and playing cards. There is a sticky smoke collecting at the ceiling from their cigarettes, and their gruff laughter echoes off the four walls. They don't notice me as I walk past to my bunk. Upon heaving myself to the top, I pull out the current novel I'm reading and settle into a comfortable position. It's challenging to focus with the loud voices of intoxicated gambling. After a few minutes, I drown them out.

"Heya!"

I flinch and my book falls to the floor.

"Oi, sorry mate," A young gentleman says, his voice lathered with Irish decent . As he kneels down to pick up my novel, he examines the cover turning it over in his rough hands. A little nosy he is. "Phantom of the Opera, huh?"

"Uh, yeah." I reply. He has to sweep his fuzzy red hair out of his eyes as he hands it back to me.

"Ner' read it." He smiles, "Haven't read a book sin school."

"That's a shame."

"Nah, I jus tell bar stories, it's bout the same. Better actually!" He laughs as if what he said was funny. Really funny, "Bertram Terrell!" He takes my hand in his and shakes it with a firm vigor. He's young, can't be older than twenty it seems.

"Frederick Tamlyn."

"Well Frederick, we seen ya all alone over her' Must be new. I was like ya too on me first cross. Jus' seeing if ya wanna play some cards." He gestures over to the noisy men in the corner. They keep their scruffy faces buried in the cards, not bothering to look over at us.

I pause just long enough to think. I can't think of something I'd rather do less, "I suppose there's no harm."

"Great!" He replies and strides back over to the smoke

clouded men. I set my novel back under the bunk and follow. All I really want to do is finish reading, is that too much to ask?

The men introduce themselves quickly and deal me a hand. Deep creases run through every card and they are as thin as a wheat crisp. Yet another indication of the lack of currency that passes through the hands of us laborers.

"Wanna smoke?" Bertram hands me a cigarette and a light before I can answer. I take a quick drag and exhale the musky vapor over my hand of cards. I fight to keep my nose uncrinkled. I never much liked smoking. I think it's grimy and the smell clings onto walls and clothing like barnacles on the hull of a ship. Under other circumstances, I would politely refuse, but it would be unwise to engage in any action that would set me apart from the rest. I should make more of an active effort to diminish any decorative vocabulary as well.

"I'll raise," I say as I try to omit the revolting taste of nicotine building in my throat.

The other players fork out some extra coin, one folds. As we play, the older men of roughly forty start talking of their wives. A couple exchange lewd photographs and take turns arguing over whose woman is more voluptuous.

"What of you new guy? Got a lady back home?"

I bite my tongue, "Oh yes, many. More than can be counted for."

The man's laugh turns into a thundering, slimy cough. Probably caused by the cigs in my opinion, though many would disagree. "Quite the ladies man, eh? Should teach Bertram a thing or two."

"Oh sod off!" Bertram Retorts. I can't hold back a quick giggle.

"It's true!" The man pushes on, "Clams up like a puppy!"

Bertram's eyes fall to the floorboards and his cheeks fade to a bashful shade of pink. It's rather adorable. Somehow, I can't imagine his struggle with talking to the opposite sex. He had no issue striking up a conversation with me. He seems like a very social lad.

"I dunno man, they're' a whole nother species. Not sure what they wanna hear from me…" His face stains a deeper red as the older men laugh at him.

"Only that yer filthy rich!"

"And the heir to the British throne and can lift 300 pounds! Gotta impress them ya know!"

The laughter peaks to a roar and I can see Bertram's increasing unease through his fidgeting fingers.

"Or you know, ask them how their day went, what they like to accomplish during free time, possibly an innocent comment on how they did their hair." I chirp in, crisp annoyance trembling on my lips. Bertram catches my gaze for a moment, exposing curiosity or confusion before looking away again.

The other men go about teasing Bertram and myself for my 'ludicrous' suggestion. Why would a lady want affirmation and attention when she can have aggression and arrogance? I refrain from any more frivolous comments, despite wanting to leap down their throats. I wouldn't want anything to backfire or let on too much of my background, lest I be discovered. I reluctantly smoke a couple more cigarettes and drink, admittedly, more than I should. My night socializing with fellow crewmen ends amicably and we all crawl back to our bunks. Well, a few of us topple over, heavy with drink. Lights are out and the grungy sound of snoring men washes over the room. For the first time since my uncouth arrival in this floating castle, I feel at ease. Comfortable with the intricate perception of myself. Peaceful sleep comes easy.

II

I am seized from my slumber by a beast - no, a force. An ear-shattering grinding ricochets throughout the four walls of the cabin like a renegade bullet. I would compare it to nails on a chalkboard, but replace the board with an inch thick steel plate and the chalk with… something foreign.

I try to focus my bleary eyes but the walls seem to tremble with that ungodly sound. Did I consume more liquor than I thought? Is that why everything is clattering around? It takes me a moment to realize the very walls are indeed trembling. So are the beds, our clothing bags, the glass of water sitting on my night stand... Everything is swaying back and forth in conjunction with the awful grinding of steel.

What the hell is going on?

I push myself into an upright position. I reach into the cover of my pillow and pull out my metal pocket watch. I strain my eyes in the pitch dark. It's no use, I can't see a thing, which makes this whole experience amplified. I would guess it to be around 11:45 p.m. As soon as I close the cap on my little clock, the grinding of metal, as well as the shaking in the room, vanish. A tense silence follows as the sound washes out of the room like the tide. I can feel the quickened pace of my heart throbbing in my chest. It's so quiet, I could hear a pin drop from a mile away.

I stare doe-eyed at the gentleman in the adjacent bunk.

"What was that?" The man whose name I am unfamiliar, asks me. As if I know any more than he does.

I return his startled stare and shrug my shoulders in response.

A few moments pass by, but they feel much longer as I rattle through my mind, searching for an explanation. It's odd. As soon as the intense shudder occurred, it's gone.

"All hands on deck!" The bellowing voice of another man rings from down the hallway. It would have sounded heroic, but instead, it seemed deflated, small. Like a titan drowning at sea.

In an instant, a commotion of over a dozen men jumping out of the bunks, quickly throwing on their uniforms, struggling in the dark until a lamp is flickered on. I follow suit, my uniform is in a neatly folded pile at the foot of the bunk. Black dress pants, a blue button-up collared coat, and black boots. All these pieces are rather large for my less than average frame, and they fold in an un-orderly fashion until I can pull them straight. I throw on my brown jacket as well, it is cold outside for an April night. I'm sure I'll appreciate this foresight later.

I rush out of the crew quarters, which is located on the starboard side, deep below in the bow of the ship. Down the hallway to the left, a set of spiral staircases that offer a direct route to the engine rooms or up to the decks. I follow everyone else.

I am grateful to be close to these stairs. This ship is so large, and I've only had four days of experience navigating its labyrinthine hallways. The senior officers love barking about

HOLD ME UP IN MIGHTY WATERS

how all deckhands should know this ship inside out. Personally, however, I prefer spending my free time exploring my
books rather than this steel leviathan.

Upon arriving on the boat deck, I can't help but notice
the unorganized confusion unfolding. Every seaman that I
can remember is up on deck, wandering about like seagulls
searching for their next meal. They gather in clusters, waiting obediently for instruction. A child's tin soldiers in sloppy
regiments. We are hastily called up here in the middle of the
night, it would be nice to be informed as to why, rather than
letting us all wander aimlessly.

After further investigation, I spot large chunks of ice scattered about the deck. A few third-class passengers are kicking the smaller pieces back and forth. I admire their carefree
disposition, it is unlike the uptight nature of the upper class
that I have the privilege of serving.

I turn my attention back to the groups of blue coats
wandering about the deck. I spot a familiar face approach-
ing from the distance. He stands tall and refined, dark hair
tucked neatly under a black hat. A stern expression glazed
over his pale face. His stature and confidence make him appear a decade older than he really is.

"Officer Murdoch!" I shout.

I jog over. Officer Murdoch is the first officer on the ship
and responsible for navigation and communications between
the Captain and crew. He was at the helm when the commotion started, so perhaps he can sort out the confusion.

He looks down on me, suspicious surveillance gleaming
through his eyes. It's inappropriate for me to speak to him
unless spoken to. I forgot about that not-so-small detail of
nautical life. The hierarchy at sea is strict, and I still have a lot
to learn to pass as an able seaman.

Instead of scolding me, he answers me. Well, kind of. "Standby, Mr. Tamlyn."

He pushes past me, almost shoving me over with his shoulder in his haste. He resumes his quick pace as if he does not notice that all eyes are on him. Off to the bridge, he goes, leaving me with no answers. I'm surprised he spoke to me at all, given the vast difference in position we hold.

As I stand in the stillness of the night, I cross my arms and hug my ribs. It really is a chilly evening, even with the absence of a breeze. My lungs burn with every inhale I take, and I feel cold numbness creep into my nose and cheeks.

"They want to test er' ability to follow orders, I reckon." The young man I met prior, Bertram, says to me. As he speaks, the fog of his breath slips away into the night. "Can't think of why else they'd wake us all up." He adds.

"What about that… noise?" I ask, choking down the high pitch in my voice, "You heard it, right?"

Bertram nods and looks a little puzzled as he recalls the event.

"That was the engine's reversing." Another officer pipes in. I can't recall his name, but he is experienced and has been sailing with the White Star Line for over a decade by now. The grey in his hair shimmers as the light of the moon falls on him.

Bertram looks back to me, but only uses his eyes to say told ya so. I, however, am still curious. That answer seems too... easy. Why would the engines reverse? We were full steam ahead. I leave the two men alone to their devices. Their conversation turns trivial; women, scotch and the like, and I have better use of my time.

I pace away, curiosity pulling me towards the railings at the edge of the deck. Despite the commotion of the crew, I can hear every tik of my boots on the wood floors. The unusually quiet ocean allows every echo to amplify. I place my palm on the railing and peer over the edge.

Over five stories beneath me, the calm waters of the Atlantic are like a millpond. The dramatic height sends a chill up my spine and makes the hair on my arms and neck stand on edge.

Human innovation has reached an all-time high in the past decade. Previous to a week ago, I had never seen a ship as grand as this. I never thought that I would end up on one either, let alone be put to work. Indeed, the circumstances of my employment are, well, unorthodox and perhaps in mild violation of the law.

With so many crew members, no one has yet to notice my minor deception. My job isn't of high importance, really I'm just another cog in the machine. I am obviously fine with this - if anything, I revel in the anonymity.

"Listen up men!" I am startled out of my inner reflections by the booming voice of Officer Murdoch.

Over a dozen of us diligently assemble around our first officer, eagerly awaiting instruction. Or more importantly, an explanation. There is an eerie quiet as Officer Murdoch formulates his thoughts behind a furrowed brow. The wrinkles on his forehead are the only indicator of age on an otherwise middle-aged face. The marks of a stressful career catching up to him.

"We have struck an iceberg," He begins. No one appears surprised, we are in a part of the ocean that is thick with bergs this time of the year, or so I've been told. Plus, this is the largest ship in the world. Unsinkable.

"Starting with Decks A and B then moving downwards, all passengers must be informed. Instruct them to put on life belts, gather on the boat deck, and prepare to board the lifeboats."

"Lifeboats, Sir?" Bertram's voice has a cool crack.

"Yes,"

There is no response from the crew, but I can feel an uncomfortable shift in the mood.

"This is just a precaution, do not incite any panic," Murdoch adds and hastily walks off, sending the rest of us scattering.

The organization of this frenzy is non-existent. No one has been trained. No one knows the endless white hallways. I see hoards of crew members poking their heads around corners, only to find that the passageway is a dead end. They scurry back and forth like obedient little mice, knocking on doors that have already been knocked on, giving unknowing explanations to passengers about the unfolding events, tripping past other crewmen in an effort to perform their ill explained duties. Everyone and everything is a hopeless clutter. I hate clutter.

As I run through this maze, it occurs to me that an emergency drill may have been a good idea. There was supposed to be one scheduled earlier today, but it was canceled due to the brittle cold. Wouldn't want to cause the passengers any unnecessary hassle. Hell, I overheard a crewman lamenting about how no one knows how to launch the lifeboats. If there ever really was a catastrophe, it would be a recipe for disaster. I suppose no one saw the need to educate the men on proper evacuation proceedings. Not on a liner like this. Oh, just listen to me -- evacuation? What rubbish.

Regardless, I need to focus on getting these rich folks up on deck. I am tasked with "getting the first-class off their posh arses" as Bertram called it since they'd take longer than the rest of the passengers. Personally, I suspect their potential investments in White Star Line may have had more to do with their preferential treatment rather than pure logistics, but it would be far from in my interests to argue.

As I bang on the 10th suite door, my attempt to match the tone I've heard from cowed bellhops and waiters across Dublin is running thin. Sleepy aristocrats eye me with disgust, displeased with my intrusion. I am merely a mosquito from their point of view. Sucking away at the contentment they built for themselves behind silver and gold. Apparently, my feigned subservience is even less convincing than my oddly proportioned uniform.

"Excuse me, all passengers are to gather at the lifeboats." I assert my imaginary authority.

"At this time of night," they sneer, "whatever for?"

"Captain's orders."

I continue through B deck, my impatience mounting with each pristine door. The scent of elegant perfume and expensive cigars mix with the fresh wax of the wood floors. Everything in this beast of man-made innovation is brand new and freshly installed for the maiden voyage. Not a piece of China has been touched yet, nor any pillow laid on. The White Star Line saved no expense in their attempt to outshine Cunard Line's last liner, the Mauretania. And it has worked, there is no ship out there that is more grand, more luxurious, or larger than this.

The room numbers begin to blend together as I elbow my way up the confused stream of people toward E deck. An image from a biology book I once saw in Trinity College flashes to mind. A fish - Americans call it a salmon - that swims upstream. I am officially a fish too stupid to swim with the current. I grin at the silly comparison.

Before knocking, I check the room number: E33. Just a few more to go. I raise my fist, but the door swings open before I even knock.

"Oh thank God!" The young woman across the threshold barely looks at me before grabbing my sleeve, "Care to explain why it's been such a nightmare getting some help? Never mind, as if you'd know." She's pulled me into the room before I can begin to sputter a protest.

Once inside, she whirls around, the messy ribbon in her hair failing to prevent her chocolate brown curls from whipping me in the face. Her rather sheer pink robe flows around her ankles as if it can not keep up with her nimble twirl.

"Oh! You again! Tanner, was it?" She inquires.

"Tannin, ma'am - I mean, Tamlyn," I stutter, "Regardless, miss, I apologize for the intrusion, but -"

"But you took 17 minutes to get here - 17 minutes, Tanly! Care to explain yourself?" I open my mouth, "Never mind, time is of the essence in a crisis, and I am in crisis, sir!"

"Well ma'am, How can I be -"

"Ms. Bowerman, sir! And I'd thank you for not forgetting again! As if our previous encounter on the bridge was insufficient for me to make an impression!"

She had made an impression - on both myself and the gentleman she was assaulting with her handbag. He was making 'improper advances'. I'm still not sure separating the two was a good idea. Would a real gentlemen step in like I did? Regardless, the altercation ended amicably, with her thanking me for putting the 'rapscallion' in his place. Said rapscallion was at least three times my age with a pocket watch chain worth more than all my earthly possessions put together. She then simultaneously introduced herself, thanked me, and told me off for disrespecting her autonomy before departing in a cloud of pomp and perfume.

"Right, Ms Bowerman -"

"Sir! I have more youth than you, call me Elsie" She grins like a cat. I have gone from a fish to a mouse.

"Elsie…" I stammer, "Captain Smith has ordered all passengers to the lifeboat launch stations, immediately."

She doesn't move.

"You need to put on your life belt and coat."

"In my bathrobe?" She huffs, "And without my mother no less! Teelyn you truly are the incorrigible sort."

"I'm sure she has already been warned. She's probably up there waiting for you."

"Warned of what?" Her previously huffy eyes turn fiery.

"Nothing to be worried about, just a minor inconvenience."

She shifts uncomfortably in her pink slippers.

"An inconvenience, indeed" She rolls her eyes, "What if I don't know where my lifebelt is?"

"Well it should be -"

"Toddy focus! You're distracting from the present calamity! My book, sir! My book!" She begins waving something in my face, "I was strolling across the room when the ship pitched violently sending myself and my book careening into this fine bottle of Canadian ice wine!" She gestures to an entirely empty bottle. "And just look! My book is ruined, entirely ruined!"

She hands me her copy of Futility: Wreck of the Titan. It does smell strongly of expensive alcohol.

"Elsie, this is a terrible book to read on a ship!" I was familiar with the novel, having read it several years prior. "A story about a tragic ship accident on a liner as lamentably named as this is simply untoward! Normally I would be saddened to see five-sevenths of a book drowned in ice wine, but your choice in literature is truly irresponsible!"

Her eyes flash, "My word… Lamentably and untoward? Five sevenths? Familiarity with nautical literature? You boast quite the education for a deckhand Talman… Give me your hands,"

I fail to recoil quickly enough.

"Soft… and delicate… Who precisely are you?"

I feel a sharp inhale catch in my throat at this inquiry and I pull my hand out of hers immediately. She's just trying to get me off guard - who's exactly who they claim to be anyway?

"Excuse me," Elsie snaps her fingers in front of my nose, "I asked you a question. Are you deaf as well?"

"I'm Frederick Tamlyn, of course."

"But who are you? Certainly not a seasoned sailor, that's quite evident."

Her intense dark eyes scan over me like a hawk, ready to snatch up any hint of deception that leaks through my lips.

"I am…" think faster! "New to this line of work." I force a smile.

A blank half-second, then an overly exaggerated sigh mixed with an oddly elegant shrug of the shoulders. She truly is a master of overexertion. I thought these upper-class women were supposed to be more refined and well mannered. "Well you're no fun," She thrusts her damp book into my hands, "and apparently a simpleton. The stains have already done irreparable damage and the print will surely run without immediate tending. I am to have it read by the time we dock in New York."

Stuffing the clearly doomed book into my coat pocket I seize my opportunity to make a timely exit "Yes, ma'am!"

And turn on my heel.

"It's Elsie!... You simp.." She half mutters. I take a step through the door, but a pang of guilt disallows my escape prior to informing this 'Princess Elsie' of the alarm. I turn back to see her tamping down a cigarette while eyeing a yet uncorked bottle of wine.

"Sorry to linger..." I say.

"Yes?" She looks up but then comes to a stop.

"But, you really should report to the decks. Just in case." A second passes and she continues to stare. A moment later she blinks hard and resumes, but with a slight change of affect - so slight it doesn't immediately occur to me what it is.

"My my, you really do take your part seriously, don't you?" She looks me up and down as if I'm naked.

"It's just my job," I say in the gruffest tone I can muster while turning to make my final exit.

"Huh, maybe..." Her tone is bemused - not unlike a school teacher upon catching a child in a hopelessly implausible string of lies "but your job or not, that uniform is certainly not yours." Her words wash over me like the freezing Atlantic. "Perhaps I was mistaken - you are fun!"

"Well miss, I must run - many more passengers to rouse!" I almost leap through the door.

"For the last time, Mr. Tamlyn" she hisses the name with pleasure, "Call me Elsie!"

A bead of sweat drips down my temple as I power walk away from room E33. The nerve! I think to myself as I round a corner and approach the next door. I only begin to notice the emptiness of the hallways as I begin to knock. Silence… well, not quite. The purity of silence is unknown to ocean liners, replaced by creaking steel and a deep thrum that emanates from the very walls. Peaceful at times, but something about the lifelessness of it all… the fact that even one's own whisper can get lost down these endless passageways.

I decide my work here is complete, and start toward the boat deck for further instruction. I pull my little pocket watch from inside my coat. 12:15 a.m. As the echoes of my foot falls blend with the omnipresent whir of the ship I imagine the irritation among passengers. There is a lot of fuss over bumping into a berg.

I don't understand. I sent so many people to the lifeboats, as did my colleagues, but there is only about a dozen people visible on the starboard side. The decks are as cold and vacant as a windy cemetery.

"Bertram!" I call to my familiar dark haired friend, "Where are all the passengers?"

"Ay, they're'n the sitting room. Too cold for that lot. Don't blame em'neither, Wouldn't be out here me'self but for Ol'Lightoller's promise to tan me arse" he jokes.

"Terrell, Tamlyn!" I jump at the voice of Second Officer Lightoller, "These lifeboats are going in the water with or without your help."

"Aye aye, sir!" Bertram calls back and hurries to Lightoller's side. I follow quietly. Why would Lightoller be launching the lifeboats? Surely there is no need.

I don't know how these things work, and by the looks of it, those rumors of ill-educated seamen are correct. A knot of men in blue coats fiddling with various ropes and ties reminds me of a school of guppies frantically nibbling at algae before the inevitable bigger fish comes along. I almost giggle, but the thought of what should occur if they fail to launch the lifeboats sends a shiver up my spine. Lightoller's boisterous commands only multiply their anxiety. They drop and fumble under his stern instruction, caught between wanting to be efficient and being forced to be quick. I grab at a loose rope, looking it over in confusion.

"Tamlyn, tighten that rope! We can't have the boat falling in the water because of poor knots-menship."

I pull on the rope with all my weight. My frozen hands burn as it fights against my grip. Lightoller is much more intimidating that First Officer Murdoch. More demanding as well. He carries himself as if he was The Captain Smith, looking down his nose with his head held high and mighty. Here stands a man for whom an order is sacred. Strictness aside, however, his instruction is clear and his very presence seems to chase away the fears I am trying to keep sealed in my stomach. We prepare the boats for launch as best as a lot of novices can muster up.

"Women and Children, come forward," Lightholler yells out.

I'm not sure who he is calling to, there is only a pair of women and their husbands standing by. They step forward cautiously, looking back at their husbands with a great deal of concern.

"This way please," Lightholler guides the women to the edge of the lifeboat that is now dangling off the edge of the great ship, many stories above the cold Atlantic ocean.

One of the women stops abruptly, planting her feet firmly on the hardwood. "I'm not getting in there."

Lightoller stares at her sternly, but when the woman returns the gaze it becomes obvious he has no other card to play.

"Neither am I," The other one huffs, "That quaint little

thing will tip over and drown us all."

"Very well ma'am," Lightholler trips over his voice and turns to face Bertram and me, "Only women and children are to be admitted into the boats. Go and see if there is more commotion on the port side." My guts churn as he turns away, mumbling to himself. For the first time, he seems to be tripping over his words and his impeccable posture is slouching as if he is coming apart at the seams.

We head out without question, grumbling to each other about the unorganization of the officers and the reluctance of the passengers.

The port side of the ship is not much different than the starboard. Confused women with their husbands stand back as Officer Murdoch attempts to lead the crew in the preparation of the boats. They have just readied it for launch when Murdoch catches sight of us.

"You two! Over here!" We jog over. "We need men to man the hatch and lower the boats," he states in an odd matter of fact tone.

Bertram is at the side of the boat in an instant. He is youthful and eager to show his value in front of the senior officer. I, being somewhat less youthful and, shall we say, less physically apt, listen obediently and walk opposite to Bertram.

Murdoch calls for another round of women and children, but none are left.

"Anyone else!" He yells and a few men step forward. I watch as they clamber over the side, easily finding a spot to sit in the half empty space. There is a moment of silence, and I catch the gaze of a gentleman. His eyes meet mine as if asking, "What is happening?" Although I can't tell if they are demanding or pleading for an answer. I look away.

"Left and right together." Murdoch declares, as confident as ever.

"Wait!" I pipe up, my voice cracking. "We're actually launching these things?"

Murdoch glances at me with a solemn tint in his gaze and gives a nod. This is madness. I fumble around with the rope and levers until I feel the boat begin to crank down. Bertram has an easier time with his crank, and one side starts to fall further than the other. The people shout and wail back at us until we level it out again. The same thing happens again, and again. Bertram lowers too quickly; I falter; the people scream. It is a dreadful attempt.

After several long, labor-intensive minutes, the lifeboat slams into the water in the most ungraceful manner, and the frightened screams of the women feels like a dagger in my chest. I wince at the sound. Peering over the side of the great liner and into the boat below, I count 28 people. The boat can clearly hold more than double that.

"Mr Tamlyn." I turn back to Murdoch. His eyes are inspecting me in a way they hadn't before.

"Yes, Sir."

"I don't recall you're insubordination on our last voyage." His tone is steady, but I pick up on the accusation hidden under the professional exterior. I fein a look of shock. "Right then, and on the decks earlier. You never questioned my command before." He raises an eyebrow, "and on top of forgetting your place, you also seem to have left about three inches of height on land."

A silence comes between us like the ocean creeping up the hull of the ship.

Officer Murdoch never takes his eyes away from me. He analyzes my every move, every glance away, the way my fingers fidget at my sides, he misses nothing. I feel a warm prickling sensation melt my cold numb cheeks. I do my best to stifle the growing color on my face but it's no use. Any onlooker can observe my discomfort.

"I would venture a guess that Frederick Tamlyn isn't really your name, is it?" He breaks the silence, and his words cut like glass.

I offer a half-hearted smile, still dumbfounded. Murdoch's stern expression doesn't falter.

"I'm not sure I understand what you're saying," I lie, "If you would like, we can discuss your concerns somewhere private."

I feel Bertram's stare on me. I'm sure he is jolted by my outright refusal to answer a direct question coming from the First Officer. I try to suppress my pending anxiety with a smile. I am playing with fire by toying with Murdoch.

"Move on to the next boat." Murdoch shouts to the by-standers, never craning his neck to look away from me, "Women and children first. Then the men."

They disperse without question, something I wish I would have done from the beginning.

If my intuitive nature would not have gotten the best of me, I would not be in a situation as imperative as this. Im-personation is sure to hold a heavy price, and I'm not willing to pay for it.

The deck is empty, Murdoch and myself are the only souls within earshot.

"You see, sir," I begin stumbling over a string of excuses, "I have injured my-"

"Enough," Murdoch cuts me off, "I know you're not Fred-erick Tamlyn."

I stay silent. It appears the story I built for myself is breaking down.

"Just tell me who you are, and make it quick." His voice doesn't sound angry. If anything, it sounds indifferent and tired. Like, there's something else weighing on his shoulders.

I allow my perfect posture to slouch and heave a sigh. I have been caught. At least it wasn't by Lightoller, I would stand no chance of an explanation if it was him.

"My name…" I trail off, my palms grow sweaty and my voice catches in my throat, "I'm Cassandra Lynch."

"Cassan-dra?" I can tell my words are lost on him. Of all things, a woman was the last person he expected me to be. "Casey, if you prefer," I add in an attempt to relieve his shock, to no avail. His eyes on me are stern for a moment before they soften into a light chuckle. His face cradles the expression of a man who can not be shaken by anything, even an uncouth imposter like myself.

"Was it the scotch that did him in?" His laugh is almost childish, "I've heard he was quite the blotto."

I feel the tension throughout my limbs lighten. "Yes, it was," I laugh as I remember the young Frederick Tamlyn stumbling into my cot with anticipation, only to be blindsided, tied up with a bedsheet, and left without clothes, credentials or hope for a job in the morning. "He made it all too easy," For a moment I speak as if bantering with a friend.

Instead of apprehending me, Murdoch just shakes his head with a small smile, "You remind me of my fiance." His eyes are far away, "She's just as unpredictable… Which is why I insist you should be in the next boat we launch. Come along."

I follow his quick strides, a little baffled at the friendliness. Is there going to be a follow-up? Am I getting arrested? Should I even ask?

"Murdoch?" I speak quietly, "Why are we launching the boats?"

He tilts his head in my direction, eyes solemn. I watch a whirlwind of emotions dance across his face like an elaborate theatre production.

"You already know," he says. "We're sinking." He shakes his head as if he doesn't believe the words coming out of his mouth.

"What?"

"Yes, yes, even I had to take a moment to reckon with the absurdity of the thing, but you're a smart young…lady. We will only be afloat for another hour or so, maybe less and you don't have a prayer as a man. So come with me and I'll make sure to get you on a lifeboat, miss."

My gaze travels from Murdoch's sad eyes down to the shiny wood floors I am standing on. Am I to believe that this will all be underwater before daybreak? "Alright." I reply cooly, not fully grasping the gravity of the situation.

"And Casey," Murdoch's voice has lowered to an ominous whisper, "Don't tell anyone, it will cause panic and more people will perish."

IV

I stand close to my First Officer, guiding women and children into the boats. They are still hesitant to board and now that I know the truth, I feel a knot in my stomach. My body starts to tremble and my blood is racing through my veins. They don't know that with every spot they leave vacant, they condemn another to freeze in the frigid waters.

"Tamlyn will oversee this boat," Murdoch states and looks to me with a glint of irony. How kind of him to ensure my survival and allow me to keep my stolen identity.

"Aye, I knew ol' Murdoch was a tad nutty." Bertram pulls me to the side, "Thinking yer an impostr. What a hoot!"

"Yeah," I force a laugh.

"Too bad fer ya, gotta' get in that little dinghy while the rest er us stay up here where it's warm."

Bertram's eyes are bright as he teases me like we are old childhood lads. Forever the funny kind. I can hardly bring myself to joke back with him. He has no idea, and it would be foolish of me to tell him. But will he live if I do? I'm not sure what to do… Of all people, I've had the pleasure - and displeasure - of meeting, Bertrams the sweetest and most innocent of them all. I'd never forgive myself if I were to be the reason for his despair.

"I can't enter this boat without my daughter!" A piercing wail rings in my ears, causing me to swing around to face the source.

"Mrs. Bowerman, please-"

"No, I won't have it. Find my Elsie at once!"

The name Bowerman sends a wave of nausea swirling around my stomach. That name used in that tone can only mean one thing. This woman must be Elsie's mother, and it's obvious that the apple doesn't fall far from the tree. I push past Bertram and approach the madwoman.

"Why isn't Elsie with you?" I inquire politely.

"My, my, what idiotic men you all are! How should I know? One minute she is rambling about a sopping book and the next she is off trying to find the seaman responsible for stealing it!"

Stealing! She practically threw the book in my face! I pause for a moment. Is it my fault that shrew isn't here? Well, not really, but if it weren't for me she'd probably been up here right now acting just as ill-mannered as her mother. "Don't worry ma'am, I'll personally go and retrieve her, just, please get in the boat. We want to maintain an orderly fashion." What am I saying?

Her eyes flash the same fiery daggers that Elsie threw at me a mere twenty minutes ago. "Fine. But, if this is not handled immediately I will have you all fired!"

"I understand," I reassure her as I lead her to the edge of the lifeboat.

"Tamlyn," Murdoch comes up to me, "We are launching, are you ready?"

My gaze flicks between the boat, Murdoch, and Mrs. Bowerman. In my mind, I can see Elsie, storming through

the halls ranting about something or other when the rivets
holding the ship together start to blow. At first, I imagine,
she would be confused, but as more and more shoot out
of the walls followed by high-pressure jets of seawater, the
confusion rapidly gives way to panic and eventually terror. I
see the terror in her eyes give way to... something else. I see
her drowning. My mind fixates on her dying eyes as the face
around them changes. Penny? Is this how my sister looked
when she fell off that peer? To be honest, I couldn't say. I
haven't seen either her or mum since they left for America six
years ago. While I know Penny isn't nine any more… wasn't
nine… it's still that childish face that's been haunting me ever
since I got that damned telegraph. The face of a child around
the eyes of death. I'm going to America to pay my respects
and hopefully exorcise this phantom - I cannot have a second. I must find Elsie.

"I can't," I fret.

I spin on my heel and barge through the small hoard of
people. Before I'm free, I feel a heavy jerk on my arm. Murdoch has pulled me back around to him.

"Casey! I can't guarantee your safety if you leave." His
voice is low and pleading.

"I know," I mutter, "Can Bertram take my place?"

"I can do my best, but I need him on the cranks. He's the
only one who can bloody run them."

"Then I wish you the best, sir! I hope to see you soon,
alive and well."

I run. Peeking back, I see Murdoch shaking his head as he
returns to his duties.

I pound on the door E33 but receive no answer. I pound
again. Harder this time. No

answer. Good God, where could this woman have run off

    HOLD ME UP IN MIGHTY WATERS

to? I swing around, exasperated at this idiotic turn of events.

I let out a few heavy breaths and focus on the pounding of my heartbeat behind my ears. These halls are deathly quiet, like the silence before the piercing wail of a banshee. As I gaze down the hallway into the bowels of the ship I feel off-balance as if the weight of my chest is being pulled forward, and every step I take is trudging upwards. It takes only a moment for the sinking realization that this is not just a trick of the mind, but reality. I am standing on a slant. I am being gradually pulled forward into the depths of the sea as the Atlantic slowly devours the steel beast. I wonder if anyone else has come to visualize the magnitude of this disaster yet.

Just as I am contemplating my course of action the floor begins to tremble. The distant thump of heavy boots echoes throughout the walls of the ship. Soon, the faint mumbles of men become loud shouts as a heap of mechanics round a corner and scurry up the corridor like rats, pushing each other out of the way as they stumble over their own feet. I jump to the side just quick enough to avoid a collision. As they pass, paying no attention to me, I note their coats are weighed down with water. All the men are soaking from head to toe. I can't imagine the series of events unfolding just a couple decks below me, and even more so, I don't want to think about what will unfold in the not-so-distant future.

Perhaps Elsie has made her way back up to the decks, or at least to the women's first-class sitting room. Surely she couldn't be doing something too irresponsible, right?

I check the first-class reception room and galley on D deck, but it, like the rest of the lower decks, is void of any life. The library on C deck is also empty, as well as the gymnasium. As if a woman like that would spend even a moment in a gym. By the time I make my way back up to A deck, I want to keel over from exhaustion. My efforts have done nothing but waste precious time and drain my energy.

I am on the boat deck once again. To my surprise, many people still have yet to understand. I see people backing away from the remaining lifeboats, fighting with the officers to stay with their families. The women and children who do board the boats do so very hesitantly, if not forcibly. I witness a young girl, approximately seven years of age, kick and scream as she is ripped from the arms of her father and gruffly handed to her mother in the boat.

"Daddy, no!" She wails as she tries to wiggle free. Her mother has her tightly wrapped in her arms and is crying as she tells her husband to be safe.

I turn away. If I find Murdoch, I can live. I'm sure Elsie has found her way into a boat by now. Besides, it's not like she has done anything kind to me. It's not like I owe her anything. What am I saying? I can't dismiss her life just because of a personal grudge. I have one more place to look, then I have done all I can and will save myself.

When I push open the golden doors to the first-class smoking room, I am hit with a cloud of nicotine smoke and the potent scent of expensive liquor. When my eyes clear and my lungs adjust, I am able to take in the immense beauty of this otherwise dirty room. The green velvet lounge chairs contrast elegantly with the red carpet. The walls are decorated with expensive stained glass portraits and intricately carved designs that dance across the mahogany. The men perusing around the room are just as expensive. High-class suits and top hats, smoking cigars that are imported from the most remote corners of the globe. These men are the very picture of the ultra-rich, and seated at a far end table with a group of these aristocrats is none other than Elsie Bowerman. Feet crossed on the table, a cigarette between her rosy lips, and a hand of poker cards in the other.

"Elsie!" I call and run over to her.

"I'll raise" she drolls to the dealer without so much as a glance in my direction. "And dear me, did you hear someone? I could have sworn I heard someone call my name, but I can't imagine anyone with an ounce of class would think it polite to interrupt our game." Her fellow card players guffaw with a degree of enthusiasm that belongs exclusively to gentlemen in the presence of alcohol and pretty young women. After pausing for the men to recollect themselves, Elsie slowly turns in my direction "Oh Tankin my dear boy," she chirps with feigned surprise " where did you come from?"

"Apologies Elsie, but we really have to go."

"Go? Go where? Have you forgotten we're on a ship?"

"To your mother! She's worried sick."

"That may be so, but I trust it to your more than capable hands to let her know I am the spitting image of health and security - beyond, actually, as I am currently taking these gentlemen for all their worth!" She takes a drag from her cigarette and grandly gestures at her, admittedly, significant winnings. Although, the way these wealthy men eye her like a hound on a bone, she could ask them for the deads to their businesses and they would hand it over with pleasure. No poker playing required.

"Yes, I see, but you don't understand-"

"No I think it's you who doesn't understand, laddy" the man at Elsie's left growls in a thick Glaswegian accent. I'm not sure how I failed to see this monster of a man before, but now that he's rising from his chair he's certainly impossible to miss. Taller than a horse and at least as broad, this Ill-tempered Scot just threw back the last of his Bushmills whiskey and is rolling up the sleeves of his oddly fashionable shirt with a precision that goes beyond disconcerting. "The miss has a game to play," he says nodding his deeply furrowed brow to Elsie, "and I believe you have a deck to swab." The other stooges at the card table laugh again but quickly become very interested in their cards.

"I apologize for any impetuousness on my behalf, sir, but her mother - "

"Oh! Her mummy! Is that it, boy? Perhaps you get weepy when away from dear ol' mum, but this fine lass is content right wher' she is."

"Naturally," chimed in Elsie, "and equally naturally, I can speak for myself."

The Scot throws her a glance as she puts out her cigarette and raises from her seat, "I'll humor him, one must give a dog a bone or they won't come back."

Elsie pushes past the gargantuan man and slips her hand in my elbow.

"Escort me like a lady." She orders.

I nod and walk her away, feeling the man's stare burn into the back of my head.

"Elsie, I really must beg your undivided attention. We are in a perilous situation and I need you to take me for my word."

"I don't know Tamlyn, you did steal my book."

"Elsie, I mean it!"

"Alright alright, if you must. But first-"

"Elsie! The ship is-"

"You forget yourself, Tammy," she says cooly "I shall return after a brief trip to the powder room. Surely you can begrudge me that?" she coos with a wink.

"Elsie, we have to go!"

"She said no, boy," I can smell the stink of scotch behind me, "I think it's time to leave the lass be."

The drunken Scott is towering over me, eclipsing my small frame. I try to hold my ground and lock eyes with him. Surely he won't go as far as to start something with a White Star Line employee. He staggers in place and balls his knuckles into large fists.

"Sir, I need you to step back, I have official business-"

"Ha!" He bellows, "Sounds to me ya tryin' to take advantage of the lass."

"I assure you, that is not the case."

The bear-like barbarian takes another gruff step at me, puffing out his chest in an act of intimidation that only a man can accomplish. His face is flushed red, either with anger, booze or a combination of both, he has to practically kneel down to get to my eye level and the edges of his impeccably trimmed mustache scratch the tip of my nose. For a first-class individual, his actions resemble that of a man seasoned in the ways of dirty bar fights and cheap ale. The spitting image of the many men I had the displeasure of meeting back in Dublin. Hardly the type of person one would associate with class and wealth.

I find myself on my arse faster than a wave crashing onto the shore. I peer up, the edges of my vision blurred by a black fuzz, and see the fat-faced drunk man with an arrogant grin, massaging his red fist. He just took a swing at me. A very good one at that. I've never been punched before, I've always been able to play my woman card whenever I found myself in a precarious situation. This ringing in my ears and throbbing pain I have yet to experience.

I place my palms at my sides and attempt to push myself from the floor, but I can't manage through the dizziness. I stumble forward and back into the floorboards. I start to taste a strong metallic flavor. What is that? With weak arms, I push up from the deck. Instantly, I feel weightless. Is it because I'm dangling off the edge of consciousness? No. I'm being forced up by the collar of my coat. He has both fists twisted into the fabric and my feet are barely touching the deck. Oh God, here comes another punch. I crinkle my face and throw my hands up in an attempt to prepare myself for the worst.

CRACK. I fall to the floor and crumple over. I become mesmerized by the red liquid pooling on the deck. Oh, that's blood. My blood. I think. The taste is stronger now and I gag, spitting a few droplets among the floorboards. To the left of me, I see shiny fragments of glass scattered around. Someone's going to cut themselves on that. It needs to be swept up.

I crane my neck in search of my assailant, feeling my head pound with every movement. I don't see him, but I hear him. He is grumbling and groaning as he kneels a couple of feet away from me. "My head!" He growls.

"That is quite enough of that!" Elsie squeals, angrier than I've ever heard her. Her voice makes my head throb harder, but that's nothing new.

The Scot grumbles something inaudible.

"Acting like a filthy peasant! Well, I've never been so offended in all my life!"

I try to focus my vision in the direction of her voice.

"Look at me when I'm speaking to you!"

She's standing with her arms crossed and looking down at the drunk. He is clutching the back of his skull with his meaty hand. Blood quickly soaking his dark hair and covering his palm. His eyes appear fearful as he looks up at an angry Miss Bowerman.

"Now I am not one for tradition, but for a man to act in such a way is a disgrace. And I'll be damned if I'm seen conversing with a disgrace."

Elsie drops the shattered remains of a wine bottle. Where did she even get that?

"M-my apologies-"

"No more!" She holds her hand up, "I am finished with you. I don't associate with scoundrels, it would tarnish my flawless reputation."

She turns away from him and he watches in awe as she leaves him keeled over and bleeding. She does not even spare him a pitiful glance.

"Tamlyn," She kneels next to me and offers a kerchief. I take it and press it to my nose. That's the first time she's ever said my name correctly. Well, my stolen name. It's a start.

"Thanks," I mumble, still distracted from my bleeding face and a pounding headache.

"Oh don't be so modest!" She giggles, "I won't tell anyone that you required a woman to come to your rescue."

I flash her a devilish smirk, the irony makes it hard to stifle the laughter building in my chest. She sure used her woman card better than I did. After a moment, I rise to my feet, still trembling with adrenaline. "I trust you to keep that a secret. Can't let my lack of masculinity slip to the ladies."

BANG! What the hell? BANG BANG! Gunshots? I whip my head out towards the port side of the deck but see nothing. I race over, keeping Elsie's hand clasped in mine, fearing she may run off and get me into another fistfight.

Second Officer Lightoller is leering over the railings, "Stay Back!"

I stand next to him, letting my gaze follow his. The white lifeboat numbered 14 was slowly being lowered into the sea.

At least this boat appears full, although there are several rafts rowing away that are only at half capacity, maybe less. As the boat is cranking downwards, I notice the water has reached the portholes along the side of the ships hull, a clear indication of pending demise. The tip of the bow is about to kiss the water, and the gradual tilt of the ship is undeniable.

They must be realizing the futility, as the crewman in charge of this boat is flailing his revolver around in a panic. BANG! He fires another round into the ocean below. People are dangling over the edge, attempting to leap into the boat. Another crewman is violently pushing passengers back with his paddle as if they were rats trying to infest their dwindling supply of cargo. I watch helplessly as a man lunges from the deck below, missing the boat entirely. He seems to fall in slow motion, his limbs flying about aimlessly until he crashes into the Atlantic. Like a fish on land, he flaps around in the water until he expends all energy and falls still.

Elsie's grip on my hand tightens.

"Tammy," She whispers. I look back to her, watching the color drain from her cheeks and a never before seen wave of fear in her eyes, "I believe we may be sinking."

"That's why I've been trying to get your stubborn arse to the boat deck. Come along, we still have some time, though not much by the looks of it."

V

Passengers are beginning to realize the danger we face. Looking out to the sea, I see that the lifeboats went from minimum capacity to almost overflowing. The boats are supposed to hold roughly sixty people. At the start, as few as twelve to twenty were the average, now the most recent boat to escape holds nearly sixty-five. Crewmen are screaming and linking arms together to stop people swarming the last boats like flies. They keep their feet planted firmly on the floorboards as men and women try to break through their barricade, despite threats of gunfire from the crew. No one cares about the firearms. They know they will die one way or another.

This angry, frightened mob is exactly where Elsie and I stand. I keep hold of her and try to push between people. Perhaps I can use my position as a deckhand to get her into one of the boats. That's the only way I can see her standing a chance. Even though she can play the woman card, with so many other women trying to save themselves and their family, it won't make much of a difference.

I struggle to push past hoards of people, and get elbowed and kicked multiple times before making it to the line of crewmen. Elsie is clung tightly to my arm. It's a fine thing that my fistfight has toughened me up.

"Bertram!" I call.

He swings his head, trying to focus on me through the chaos, eyes wide and fearful, "Frederick!"

"Where's Murdoch?"

"Bloody hell, if I know," He huffs, "He's already launched his boats. I reckon he's up untyin the collapsable's."

"Right, can you get Miss Bowerman into this lifeboat?" I forcefully pull Elsie forward, she stumbles over her feet and barely recovers herself.

"It's already launcin', I'm afraid this one's the last."

"Come On!" I hiss, "Just throw her in there!"

"It's over capacity!" Bertram has to raise his voice for me to hear over the panicked people, "Besides, if we let one in the rest will swamp the boats…I'm sry'"

"Shit…"

"Frederick…" I feel Bertram's hand on my shoulder and he presses his face close to mine so he can whisper, "We really are goin down, aren't we?"

I pull away just enough to look at him. My chest feels as cold as the ice that ripped out the rivets of our false sanctuary. I don't have to answer, the expression I carry is enough. Bertram's eyes start to water slightly as he looks around at the passengers. Some patiently wait for a lifeboat that doesn't exist, others curse, scream, and more and more have resorted to leaping from the safety rail into the frigid waters hoping to clamber onto a boat nearby.

"I'm not ready to die." He confesses, a crack in his thick, Irish accent.

"Is anybody?"

"I know it's selfish, but I want to live. I-I've never loved a fine lass. I want to marry er and have a family. I don't want to die a nobody-"

"You aren't a nobody," I cut in, "And you're not dead yet."

"But soon…"

Seeing Bertram in this desperate, panicked state really causes the depth and tragedy to settle. This event will spare no one. She will take no pity, and grant mercy to none. Not even a young, almost twenty-year-old. At his age, he is considered a grown man but has yet to experience the freedom of life that men do. Now he's trapped. I can't bear to speak the unnerving truth that he will most likely never be free again. There's a decent chance that the rest of us won't have the luxury of spreading our wings either.

"Oh, Bertram," My voice cracks and I find myself wrapping my arms around his shoulders. I have to stand on my tiptoes for the embrace, "Whatever happens, you are an honorable man."

My cheeks brush along the stubble from his chin and I can't help but admire the scent of subtle, cheap cologne. Even as a deckhand, he takes pride in his labor and appearance.

"As a woman, I think you are a delight and would be an easy man to love," I add in a hushed whisper, as not to divulge my identity to bystanders. I doubt anyone would care at this moment, but I always stick to my story.

His eyes scan me over with odd precision. I see the confusion written over his face before my revelation sets in. His cheeks and nose flush a crimson red as he darts his eyes away and covers his mouth with his hand.

"I'm so sorry," He says, "I treated you like one er the lads. Our talks wer', not good fer a lady."

"Then I played my part well," I laugh with empty humor, letting my feminine tone breakthrough.

He shakes his head and chuckles uncomfortably, "What a terrible time fer this to come out, it'd been nice ter know the real… what's your name?"

"Casandra Lynch. Casey."

"Casey," He says my name like it's a foreign object, "Try en get to a collapsible, we'll try to keep order here."

Bertram gestures to let us through the barricade of frightened seamen. I push Elsie through, to which she protests my less-than-gentle handling of her. I latch on to Bertram's hand as we pass. "Come with us."

His chocolate eyes meet mine and his bushy brows contort in frustration. "I can't." He shakes his head, "There are still so many other lasses like yerself' It would be a crime against God to save myself before them. I'd rather die tryin' to save souls than live knowin' I left em."

My eyes water as I scan his youthful face.

"You're an honorable man, Bertram. Take care of yourself. Thank you."

He blinks away the tears collecting under his eyelids and gives me a warm smile, the last of his I'll probably ever see.

"You too, Casandra."

I hold back the tears gathering in the corner of my eyes, choke back a sob and rush off with Elsie. Several yards down the deck, I spot Murdoch and a few other men struggling with an emergency collapsible. How ironic that they have emergency lifeboats, yet still not enough for half of the passengers. Murdoch has all his weight pushed into the boat, but it does little more than rock back and forth. As I approach I see the exasperated look on his face and his dark hair is wet with sweat.

His expression turns sad when he sees me, "Cas- Tamlyn."

"Let me help," I call to Murdoch, and turn to Elsie, "Please wait right here."

I use the rickety ladder to climb on top of the officer's quarters. The boats are tied securely to the roof, away from passengers walking the promenade decks. In hindsight, it's out of the way and a terrible place for quick access.

"Grab this side, we're going to have to try and slide it off." Murdoch orders. I comply and give the great boat a mighty heave, feeling it budge forward slightly.

"Wait!" I stop, "we need ores to help break the fall. Elsie! Here!"

I drop my side and grab a few ores from the bottom of the emergency raft. I walk over to the edge and stare down at a very well dressed Elsie.

"Catch these," I tell her.

"I beg your pardon!" She begins to protest but I toss the ores in her direction before she can say more. She catches them with an elegance that can only be described as an elephant falling, dropping them awkwardly on the floorboards and stumbling backward.

"These need to be set alongside the walls."

She blinks back with a stare, challenging me to order her around again.

"So the boat can slide down, it may break if we don't."

She eyes the ores with disgust as if the physical assertion is beneath her. At that moment a terrible shudder ripple throughout the deck of the ship, and we all vibrate with the power of 52,000 tons being tossed about like a bag of feathers. I have to lean on the boat to steady myself. The ship jerks and slides forwards at an alarming increase of speed. My eyes fall down to the bow, and I witness an astonishing, blood-curdling sight. The bow is no longer visible. Vanished. It has been replaced with a black layer of water, and the ocean is stalking up the decks like a hungry predator. Lord knows how much time we have left on this steel behemoth.

"Done!" Elsie shrieks. I'm guessing she suppressed her aristocratic tendencies and the fear of imminent demise motivated her to get off her posh arse.

"Good good, now stand back!"

"Hurry, Tammy!"

The water has crept up several yards. The portholes on the hull begin to burst one by one as the pressure of the water builds. The great ocean liner, the finest of her time, is now plunging under, never to be seen again. She will take thousands down with her. I try not to took at the people flopping about in the water, or wonder about those trapped in the lower decks.

Murdoch and I count to three and heave with all our might, willing the lifeboat to move. We struggle again. And again. Finally, we have shuffled it to the very edge and, as gently as possible, attempt to slide it down the makeshift ore ramp.

The boat seems to float over the edge as Murdoch and I continue to push. Slowly, I feel the resistance of the raft give way. It falls off with a loud crunch. Looking down, I see the remains of ores that were split in half. The weight was too much and it split and crushed the ores that made up our ramp.

"Shit!" Murdoch growls.

The boat has also flipped. It sits upside down on the quickly disappearing deck. My heart plummets to my stomach. There's no way we will be able to get that the right side up before we go under. I hop off the platform next to our floundered lifeline. Murdoch lands next to me.

"Well, that was smooth!" Elsie yells.

"Just get over here and help us flip it."

"What! You have got to be fibbing with me."

For a moment, I think she will refuse, but with a theatrical groan, she places her pristine fingers around the lip of the overturned vessel and pulls with us. This odd woman still has the audacity to exert her aristocracy in a time of desperate circumstances. I am honestly a little impressed at her blatant disregard for the situation at hand. I try not to think about how I may end up losing my life over such a thick-headed woman.

Our efforts to flip this thing are in vain. Even with a few more crew and passengers crowding it, the weight mixing with hysteria proves too much. The water is only a few feet away from me now, and the mighty ship is tilted at approximately 40 degrees if I had to estimate. No one can doubt her demise now. It's only a matter of time. Minutes. I can't help myself from scanning the crowd of people, hoping my gaze may fall on Bertram. If he is still here, I can't pick him out. The remaining passengers are bunched together like sardines as the great liner slips deeper and deeper into the Atlantic.

"We're going to have to float it off," Murdoch says, "When the water gets to us."

"Alright, Elsie come here!"

"Do not call to me as if I were a mangy mutt," She growls as she steps forward, tripping over her heels due to the dramatic slant. All things considered, she is rather composed… Or daft.

"I believe you're the one who called me a dog, besides, you're more like a pampered Poodle."

She shoots me an icy glare, trying to gloss over our impending doom with her exotic flavor of humor. I hold out my hand and she takes it gingerly. I help her onto the overturned raft as if it is a front-row seat to the opera. She squats in the middle with a sort of awkward grace as she smooths out her lace and bead dress around her.

"Your turn." Murdoch stands behind me, clutching my waist and arm as he shoves me onto the raft.

"All those people are going to swamp us," I mumble.

Murdoch looks at me with sad eyes. We will only be able to allow a handful of people on, the rest will be pushed away. It's a cruel game of survival. The water is now lapping at the nose of our raft, inching ever so closer.

A deathly sound of warping metal rings in my ears. We turn our heads to its origin. The front funnel. I see only a few of the wires holding it together snap one by one. Pop, pop, pop, and disappear into the sea. Silence. Then the great chimney lurches forward, slow at first as it builds speed. As if watching a play, the massive heap of metal plummets into the sea. A mighty crash of one hundred tons sends a massive wave careening up the deck, destroying all in its path. We are in the center of that path.

I look into the wide, frightened stare of Murdoch as the water engulfs him. I shoot my arm out and clasp his hand in mine. The force of the water pulls him under, dragging me as well, but I keep steady. I feel our lifeboat rises as it floats on top of the water. I yank back with every ounce of muscle in my frail arms, trying to bring Murdoch back to the surface. Despite the pull of the water, I've almost succeeded. His hand is within sight, and soon the rest of him will be safe up here with me as well. The raft shakes violently as a swarm of passengers try to fight their way on board. In their panic, I am elbowed with such a force that only a fear possessed person can muster. I am thrown off my feet and over the edge.

I wail at the cold caress of ice water, sucking the salty sea into my lungs. The water is like a pile of needles as it rushes over me, piercing my skin. The shock forces the grip I have on Murdoch to loosen. His hand slithers out of mine like an eel and I desperately wave around underwater. To no avail. Get to the surface, I have to get to the surface. My limbs feel lifeless as I push my way to the star speckled sky above. With every motion, my muscles scream for me to get out of the frigid cold.

My head bursts through the waves and I am greeted by screams of the dying. The cry of people in pain is like nothing I've ever heard. People who know they are freezing to death, but wail and fight to stay alive. I am one of them. My arms flail about recklessly and I am gasping for breath, unable to hold back my terrified yowls. The ice feels like a weight crushing my chest and compressing my lungs into shriveled prunes. I whip my head around the field of splashing people. Where is Murdoch? I don't see him. He couldn't have gone far… unless the suction of the ship pulled him under. Did Elsie get thrown off too? Oh god, all the fancy clothing she was wearing would have pulled her under for sure!

Somehow in my delirium, I spot the overturned lifeboat. I make out over a dozen silhouettes of men standing atop it, but I can't pinpoint if Elsie is one of them. Forcing every bit of strength I have, I will my arms to paddle, but I can't tell if they are moving. Every bit of my core is tightened and every motion sends an intense burning sensation throughout my body, like a knife being dragged across my skin. My shoulders and lips tremble violently as I get colder and colder. I must be making some progress, however. The boat is getting closer and I see I am not the only one clambering to the life raft. This could pose a problem.

My hands, which have a bloodless tint of blue, grab onto

the edge of the boat. I feel my lungs giving out, and it takes more and more energy just to inhale. I try with every fiber of my being to pull myself up, but I can no longer move. I have to look intently at my arms to be sure that they are still attached to my torso. I pull, and pull some more only to slip and fall under the waves. I don't know if I can find the motivation to pop my head back up. Another painful gulp of seawater persuades me to try again. The current caused by the flailing limbs of others gives me just enough of a push to the surface, but staying afloat is a feat I can't endure.

"Stay back!" I hear the distant scream of someone familiar. Lightholler? My vision is

blurring so I can't make out if it's him, but I feel a hard force shove me back, out of reach from the boat. The end of an ore is forcing me back underwater. No, I can't swim back. I'm too cold.

"No! Stop that at once!"

"Ma'am stay back, it's not safe-"

"Remove your hands at once!"

"Mi-"

"At once!"

That voice… Elsie? I guess I'd recognize her defiant screeching anywhere. I feel a hand on the collar of my coat as it floats me to the edge again. I am being tugged upwards, but I can do little more than act as an anchor. I don't even raise my arms, I just bob in the ocean.

"C'mon Tammy, you've got to help me out a little bit…"

The tugs on my coat become lighter as Elsie loses energy and pants.

"He's done for miss… and we are out of room."

"No!"

"That's Frederick!" A shivering voice rings in my ears.

That voice… Harold Bride? Did he really make it out of the wireless room? "Pull him up! He's got e-enough will power, he'll make it!"

I'm not done for, I'm alive. I let out a pitiful groan and use every bit of willpower to thrust my arm into the air. I feel a firm clasp on my wrist whom I can only estimate as Harold's, and I grip back with all the might of a mouse. My shoulder is pulled up onto the side of the raft and I feel a second hand on my back. I kick or imagine myself kicking, to help myself onto the overturned boat. Suddenly, my body feels even chillier than before as the air hits it. A venomous shiver ripples down my spine, and I curl into my knees, unable to control my vicious trembling and chattering teeth. I feel fingers run over my wet, ice-coated hair. My vision is all but a tiny tunnel as my body does everything possible to conserve the remaining heat. I am disoriented as my head is raised and set on something cold and cushy. I can't pick apart what it is. The fingers continue to run over my hair.

"Hang in there Fredrick," Harold's voice is hardly audible in the distance, "We were able to send that message before…"

I can't articulate a sentence, I can't focus on much else, and I can't move a muscle. I try to huff a reply and then settle on trying to count how many times the boat sways back and forth, but I lose track at two. I fight to stay awake. I feel sleepy. So sleepy…

"That's it, he's gone."

Whos gone?

"We've waited long enough, I'm so sorry…"

Have we been rescued? My eyelids have frozen shut and I don't have any feeling or control in my limbs. I try to lift my head, but nothing moves. The collar of my jacket is roughly heaved upwards, followed by an ear-shattering scream and a loud smack.

"If you lay one hand on him I will throw every last one of you heathens in the water and kill you all!"

God almighty, I hope I never meet that woman. She could send a lion packing for the hills by the sound of it. The others must have that conclusion as well, there is not another word from the intimidated men. Why is it so cold? I hope we can all sit by a fire with a cup of hot chocolate soon - or better yet, a glass of spicy whiskey. With much strain, I manage to twitch my fingers. That's a relief, I was starting to wonder if I still had hands, or arms… or feet for that matter. My feet! Do I still have them? I can't feel them.

A wave of darkness descends on me before I can answer that question.

I'm a great deal dryer than I last remember. A few extra layers have been draped over my shoulders as well. My eyelids comfortably flutter without that layer of ice that had crusted on them. I wiggle my feet as well which gives me a great deal of comfort. I had a dream that I lost them, my hands as well.

The sky is painted a pastel pink as the sun creeps over the ocean line. I am lying face-up on some old hardwood floor. I can't help but feel very off, and very unaware. I just experienced the grandest ocean liner in the world break apart and give way from under me. Right? My lightheadedness would suggest otherwise.

"Dear God Tammy." A familiar voice sighs, "could you have been anymore hopeless?"

I stare at her, she looks disgruntled. Her chocolate curls flay in odd directions and her expensive dress stained and wrinkled.

"On the raft," She continues in a tone that hints at my

daftness, "Everyone thought you deceased. They tried to toss you over like the others, but I knew you weren't. You could have helped me out a little, caused me a handful of trouble you did."

"My apologies, Elsie."

"You should be," She huffs, "I've had to save your arse about a dozen times."

The way 'arse' slips from her lips sends a giggle through me. It's very unbecoming of someone in her class, yet it perfectly illustrates her deviant demeanor.

She is very talented at making small talk, but I can see that her smile does not reach her eyes. She is only putting on a farce. Not that I can blame her. "So… How bad is it?" I ask the question.

She pauses and allows her smile to drop and her eyes to fall to the floor. "They believe the death toll to be over one thousand. Captain Smith was lost. My mother is safe, praise the Lord. I don't know of your friends, Tamlyn. You will have to check the list for them, but it doesn't sound hopeful. The worst casualties were the crew... That Harold fellow, he lived. Badly crushed feet, but alive. He helped me pull you onto the raft. The other operator… I can't recall his na-"

"Jack Phillips,"

"Mr. Phillips… Was on the raft as well, but he perished from exposure shortly before our rescue… I'm sorry,"

I stay silent as I remember the excitement those two men shared while they picked apart the broken telegraph only a day prior. I suppose they fixed it… Otherwise we would still be floating aimlessly in the ocean.

"What of Murdoch?"

Elsie's eyes water as she meets mine, I know the answer before she speaks, "Gone."

I breathe out a long sad sigh. In my heart, I knew the moment I lost his hand underwater that I would never see him again. As much as I know that it's not my fault, that none of this is my fault, it's hard not to feel guilty. If I had just held on a little tighter or worked harder to get the raft in the water…

"I'm sorry, Tamlyn." Elsie's tone is smooth and considerate.

"He was a good man, they all were." I say, "It's a tragedy that none of them deserved to die for."

"There will be serious repercussions for this." Elsie's voice has done a 180 and turned from soothing to menacing, just like the cat and mouse game she played on the ship, "This will go down in history as the worst nautical disaster of the modern-day. I'd be surprised if White Star Line ever launches a successful ship ever again."

"That doesn't fix what's been done. It doesn't bring anyone back."

"It sure helps mend the wound, however." She snarls, the crease in her perfectly sculpted brow giving way to anger and ferocity that heats the space between us. "I want nothing more than to see some justice."

I nod. I don't have a vindictive nature, but she's right. This should not have happened. There's so many steps that could have been taken to avoid catastrophe. Safety protocol that was intentionally amiss and a lack of lifeboats are only a start.

"I need to see the passenger list," I state as I get to my feet, feeling wobbly.

"It will only upset you, you should at least rest first."

"I have to know."

"Fine. Do as you will, but I'll be accompanying you."

I don't bicker with her about this. I don't mind her company. Of course, that could be the near-death experience talking, prior to this I wanted nothing more than to escape her condescending remarks.

We walk off to the nearest crewman on deck. Scattered along the floor of the ship, Carpathia I believe, are huddles of people bundled together in blankets. There is a silence among all of us. The unimaginable loss of life that occurred has slipped away. There is nothing that remains to give light to the event other than our own stories. The ocean is as vast as it always was. The waves reminiscent of a millpond, just as they were when She plunged under them.

"May we see the list?" I ask a young steward.

"Y-yes, of course." He fumbles with the papers in his hands, "Whom are you looking for?"

"Bertram Terrell. Crew."

The steward's eyes look at me with pity, then he flips through his pages.

"Not on the list... Sorry."

"I see… Thank you."

I turn away. I wasn't expecting him to live, he made it very clear that his place was helping the others. I had hoped, though, that somehow he made it out of the thousands of drowning people.

We are to be arriving at the New York Harbor within the hour. After three days of mostly dim silence at sea, our adventure is to come to an end. Or so I like to think it will. I know that there will be inquires and formalities to disclose. I'm not worried about that. It's the idea that life will go on and this whole ordeal will be lost to the imagination. There will be an uproar of course. I'm sure we will be swimming in news publications for months to come, starting when we step foot off the Carpathia. But after that, this will all just be a story. The realness of it will fade and be forgotten. I doubt many will remember the names of us. No one will hear the story of Bertram Terrell and his devotion, nor will they hear of Elsie and her temperament. Murdoch's name may very well be smeared, for he was at the helm when we hit. Only time will tell how we will be remembered, but we all have a way of looking at the world through a cynic's spectacles.

But I fear that one day, This will all be gone and forgotten.

"What do we do after this?" Elsie asks as we look out to sea, a small blur of America on the horizon. She has been hanging around me for the past few days, despite her mother's disapproval. She has a much brighter attitude, given the circumstances.

"I'm not sure." I respond, "Live I suppose."

"Well obviously. But how do you plan on doing that?"

"... I'm going to visit my mother. I'm not sure she will want to see me, however."

"Well she better." She huffs, "Despite your sudden bursts of rudeness, you are quite a delight."

"My rudeness?"

"Yes, you are quite the handful."

"Well, I have something to apologize for my 'outbursts' as you call them."

Her eyes dart around me before fading into a mischievous smile, "What makes you think I could want anything you have to offer me?"

I ruffle through my borrowed, dry coat pocket and pull out a wrinkled clump of poorly dried paper bound in an equally damaged hardback cover.

"My book!" She seizes it from my hand before I can formally hand it over. "My, my" She tisks as she flips through the pages, "You sure did tarnish the poor thing, it's completely ruined!"

It was ruined well before it came into my possession.

"I'm kidding, of course." She reassures, "You really need to learn how to take a joke."

"You should tell better ones."

She flashes me a devilish, threatening grin before fumbling through the ruined pages once more.

"I suppose that will be a relic someday." I continue, "So, where will you go now?"

"To Alaska with my mother. My father had business up there, and since he passed when I was young, we decided it would be beneficial to experience what he left behind." She sounds mechanic.

"Is that all?"

"Oh no. I have visions of grandeur! All my ideas and passion cannot go to waste! There is much work to be done on the homefront - the homefront being equal rights."

I try to speak, but she silences me with a finger wave and shushes.

"Take you and me for example. Clearly, I am more rational and intellectual. Yet in all aspects of society, you would be given favor on behalf of the extra weight in your groin."

I feel the heat rush out of my facial pores and I whip my head around. I hope to the Lord that was not overheard. I don't think I'll survive another drunken fistfight.

"Oh calm down Tamlyn. No one can hear us. Besides, you've been present in more lascivious conversation in the cigar room, no doubt."

"W-well, I was just caught-"

"Young men always try to play coy. They think we are daft to debaucherous behavior, the fools."

"I'm not sure how to reply, but I would be grateful if you kept your voice down…"

"Ah Tammy, you can be quite adorable when you're flustered."

"Quit being salacious, it's unbecoming."

She giggles a bit. I suppose she sees me as less of an employee now, and I'm unsure whether that's for better or worse.

"You insist I call you Elsie, but have only ever regarded me by my last name. Why?" I ask, steering our banter to a more appropriate topic.

"Truly... I forgot your first name."

"Really?"

She nods. "Enlighten me."

"Casandra." I reply without forethought, "My bad! How silly, I meant to say... Franklin- Frederick!" I crash my eyelids shut and shake my head quickly. I allowed myself to break character for only the slightest of moments. With a heavy sigh, I open my eyes again and flinch at Elsie's direct stare. I wait for the shocked, even appalled expression to wash over her face. It doesn't. She blinks once and breaks out in a radiant, yet arrogant smile.

"I knew you were fun!"

"You... Excuse me?"

"When you were fumbling about my stateroom like a frightened puppy, I knew you had something to hide. Quite a fun little game you played. I must say, I didn't fathom a... woman? Shame on you!" Her voice shifts from delighted to defensive.

"I'm sorry..?" All rhetoric has caught in my throat as I try to keep up with her pace.

"Shame on you, Tam- Cassandra!" She growls, "I was growing to admire you - I dare say I was almost smitten!"

My face flushes and my body feels as if it's concaving. "I-

I-”

"Smitten Cassandra!" Her words slap me in the face, "Here I was taking delight in the fantasy of-of an Irish spy escaping his treacherous past. Or-or a poor man desperately attempting to slither into an aristocratic lifestyle by wooing a young, beautiful member of the elite!"

"I can hardly be held responsible for your desires-"

"Desire! No no, it was mere fantasy."

I think I'd like to be thrown back into the Atlantic.

"No matter." Her voice calms to an aggravated hush, "It was a rather foolish thought."

I swallow the bile building in my throat and release a timid sigh. "You're fantasy- I mean assumptions are not too far off however. My family came from lesser means and I was a student at Trinity, Dublin, "

"And what has come of that?" Elsie seems only mildly distracted from the previous topic.

"Nothing yet." I state, "I left as soon as I received a telegram from my mother."

"Well go on." She demands after a moment of silence.

"You see…" I struggle to find words to explain my situation, "My mother and little sister emigrated a few years ago. The American dream and what-not. Our good-byes were less than amicable - I fought tooth and nail for her blessing to remain in Dublin. The opportunities for education were much more progressive there than in the States. She disagreed, adamant that family was to come first. They left, I stayed and we have not spoken since."

"So you fancy a reunion..? That telegram must have weighed quite a bit."

"No." My breath shortens and my eyes begin to sting, "It said, 'Penny has passed. Fell off a pier and drowned.' Nothing more."

Elsie grabs my hand and gives it a squeeze, "I'm sorry to hear."

"It's been rough." I admit. "My Penny is-was very dear to me. It hurts to think that the last she ever saw of me was screaming at her beloved mother."

"Sounds like you still hold some animosity."

"Of course. Mother was selfish and overbearing. We had opposing beliefs about everything. Nonetheless, we are not immortal and I don't wish for my mother to pass with not a soul who cares for her. Penny was her whole life, much more than myself, and if I can rebuild a fraction of kin hood that will be enough."

"You're a tad braver than I thought," Elsie purrs, "I can commend anyone who forgets everything for the wellbeing of the family. However, I implore you to go back to school. You have potential, and it would be a shame to see it wasted on arbitrary duties. In the end, it's about your life and no one else's."

"I didn't realize you were a motivational speaker." I try to push away my growing discomfort with a snide remark.

"Of course. I am an activist and campaign all around the world. I hope to be a lawyer in parliament someday. That is, when women are legally permitted to do so."

"I'm sure it's only a matter of time."

"They can't deny us forever." She replies, "My how we have spun wildly off-topic. Trying to distract me I see. A woman dressed as a man - a relatively handsome one at that. What else is there?"

"There's no more to it than that…"

"Rubbish. There is a week-long discussion to be had about this… But we can save it for another time. The statue of

Liberty is in sight and I need to take the last few minutes of our journey to freshen up. Lord knows there will be cameras, news reporters and the like! I must look my best."

"Alright, Elsie," I reply as she steps away from the balcony of the ship.

"Cassandra," She pauses, my name still foreign on her lips. "Do you fancy a coffee in the morning? Or perhaps a glass of wine in the evening?"

"Either… is fine." I didn't expect her to want much more to do with me.

"Both it is!" She beams, "Insatiable as you are, I look forward to it. The docks at 9:00 am precise. Don't be late. I must hear more of the honorable Cassandra… What's the latter?"

"Lynch."

"Miss Lynch, I will see you in the morrow."

She twirls on her heel and struts with a pip in her step and her nose held high. I wonder if she is desensitized to the world or simply resilient. Though I must admit, a day with Elsie Bowerman seems much less frightening now than it did only days ago. I dare say I'm looking forward to it.

I gaze out to the piers as we drift by the symbol of the United States, her copper stained torch raised high above us. Yet another reminder of how small we are, how small I am. The hustle of the city rings louder in my ears, there is no doubt that a crowd of citizens will be frothing to get a glimpse of the tragic survivors. The ordeal still hasn't settled. Now that I pause to collect myself, I'm finding it difficult to piece the events together. As if it never really happened.

I slide my fingertips over my stained blue crewman's jacket paying close attention to the golden buttons. This is the only physical memory I have remaining. There are changes of clothes just a deck below me. I could obtain proper women's attire - even if they would not be keen to give it to me, of course I have my ways around that. Or I could remain as I am. I could continue as Frederick Tamlyn - or any masculine name I appropriate. My anonymity has never been more secure than it is right now among the wreckage. My life is entirely mine to take and build upon. I can recreate myself however I see fit, and I can become whoever I fancy. I will go back to school, become an advocate of sorts. Change things for the better. Now that I know mortality is fleeting, I must make the time I have left count.

Murdoch mentioned his fiance to me. Perhaps I can start by sending her a letter. I'll tell her of her husband's courage and his dedication to his crew, myself included. I anticipate his name getting smeared, among many others. There always has to be a scapegoat. His fiance deserves to know the true tale of William Murdoch, and how he saved countless lives. It's the least I can do.

VI

Carpathia has docked at pier 54 in New York City. All the passengers have exited the ship, but here I stay. Writing out draft after draft of the letter I wish to send for Murdoch. Black scribbles stain the paper as I struggle to articulate my thoughts and droplets of my tears have soaked through, causing what few words I have to run. He's gone. They're all really gone. Bertram too. How can that fuzzy-headed goofball really cease to exist? I could have saved him too, but he didn't want that… Then again, I couldn't even rescue Murdoch when he was in my grasp. I use the sleeves of my coat to wipe away the increasing number of tears and snot leaking out.

"Excuse me?"

I barely comprehend the voice as it settles next to me. I inhale and try to force my grief back into the pit of my stomach. I turn. A pair of dark eyes, probably as bloodshot as mine are scanning over my face. I watch the smidge of hope in them die.

"I apologize," He says, "I thought you wer' someone else."

I give him a sorrowful look and the tears start to well under my eyelids again. I turn my head from him, I just need a little time to collect myself. He doesn't walk away.

"I spose' we all lost someone… Yer not the only one."

His words are smothered with the accent of an Irish man, like many of the passengers aboard. I glance him over again. A crew jacket, slightly different than my own, short dark hair is a tad messy. His nose is pointy, but his attentive expression is friendly. I bet if he had the energy to smile, it would show brightly in his eyes as well.

"You're right, I suppose there's some kind of comradery we can all share."

"Especially among us," He gestures to my attire.

"I'm actually not crew…"

"oh, I saw the coat and jus' assumed"

"It's alright, It was given to me by a very kind gentleman," I lie. I don't think I want to continue my facade any longer.

"Who did you lose? If you don' mind me asking…"

"Friends… Really good friends"

"I lost friends as well… And my brother. He would have been wearing the same coat you are. I saw ya and thought that maybe…"

"I'm sorry…"

"Can I get your name?"

I pause, thinking about how to answer.

"Casandra Lynch," I can see his expression change. I still don't have the standard appearance of a woman. He places his hand in mine and gives it a gentle shake.

"I'm Frank Terrell,"

I feel the warmth in my cheeks drain and I examine him with close precision. I see it. They have the same warm eyes, and if Frank's hair was longer it would have the same texture as Bertrams. I start crying. I wrap my arms around his shoulders and to my surprise, he returns my embrace.

"Bertram," I try to choke back a sob, "He was my friend.

He wouldn't come with me when I tried to help him. Wasn't going to abandon the others…"

I catch his sorrowful eyes as lets me go, "He was like that," Frank says, "That's why I didn't think he made it, but I had hoped…"

"So did I,"

We stand there in silent solitude, recalling the raw memories of the recent tragedy.

"I would like to hear more about Bertram and your family if you don't mind. Perhaps we can meet up for a walk in the coming days." I suggest, knowing it a little uncouth for us to meet after such a sudden introduction.

"Alright," He replies after a moment of thought, " I would like to hear more of what happened to my brother at the… end."

"Of course,"

I write down the address of my mother's house and instruct Frank to meet me there the day after tomorrow. I contemplated having him accompany Elsie and me to tea… But I'm not sure if I want to scare him off just yet. We exchange amicable farewells and I am left standing alone on the deck once more. I'm sure I'll be asked to leave soon, I'm just not sure how ready I am to move forward.

I let the air from the city waft through my hair and say goodbye to the crisp scent of seawater. Looking out to the ocean, I imagine my life back in Europe and how different it all will be now. Will I ever go back? It's hard to say. Whatever I do from here, I'll do so with unprecedented ambition. I've been blessed with the opportunity to continue living, something I hadn't given much gratitude for in the past. I'll make the most out of this second chance, but first things first.

I need to get off this bloody ship and onto dry land.

Made in the USA
Coppell, TX
03 October 2020